This Walker book belongs to:

_____

_____

_____

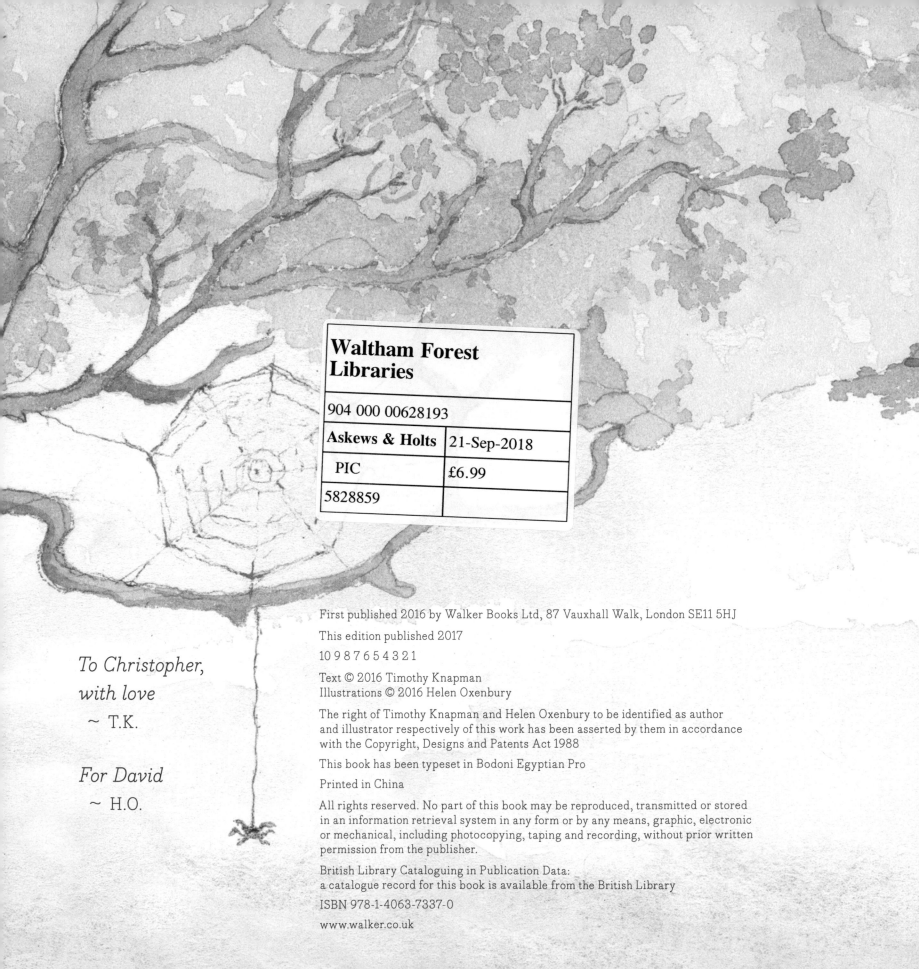

To Christopher,
with love
~ T.K.

For David
~ H.O.

First published 2016 by Walker Books Ltd, 87 Vauxhall Walk, London SE11 5HJ

This edition published 2017

10 9 8 7 6 5 4 3 2 1

Text © 2016 Timothy Knapman
Illustrations © 2016 Helen Oxenbury

The right of Timothy Knapman and Helen Oxenbury to be identified as author
and illustrator respectively of this work has been asserted by them in accordance
with the Copyright, Designs and Patents Act 1988

This book has been typeset in Bodoni Egyptian Pro

Printed in China

British Library Cataloguing in Publication Data:
a catalogue record for this book is available from the British Library

ISBN 978-1-4063-7337-0

www.walker.co.uk

Time Now to Dream

Timothy Knapman   *illustrated by* Helen Oxenbury

WALKER BOOKS
AND SUBSIDIARIES
LONDON · BOSTON · SYDNEY · AUCKLAND

Alice and Jack were out
playing catch when they heard
something that sounded like…

Ocka by hay beees
unna da recees

"What's that noise?" said Jack.

"It's coming from the forest,"
  said Alice. "Let's go and see!"

"But what if it's the Wicked Wolf?"
  said Jack. "I want to go home."

"Shhh," said Alice.
"Everything is going to be all right."

  And she held Jack's hand.

Alice and Jack were stepping into
the forest when they heard something
that sounded like...

Offtis or eeef edd
un gentil daa breeze

"What's that noise?" said Jack.
"I don't like it."

"Let's go and see," said Alice.

"But what if it's the Wicked Wolf,"
said Jack, "with his big bad claws?"

"Shhh," said Alice.
"Everything is going to be all right."

Alice and Jack were creeping through
the forest when they heard something
that sounded like...

Ime now to reem
ing de taaars in a sky

"What's that noise?" said Jack.
"We're lost!"

"It's just over there," said Alice.
"Let's go and see."

"What if it's the Wicked Wolf,"
said Jack, "with his big bad claws
and his snap-trap jaws?"

"Shhh," said Alice.
"Everything is going to be all right."

"I want to be home," said Jack.
"I want to be warm and wearing my pyjamas.
I want to be snuggled down deep."

"We have to be brave," said Alice.

And that's when they heard it,
very close now.

Sossay to leeep
on mie eeeet ullaby

"It's right in front of us!"
said Jack.

Big bad claws ...

snap-trap jaws ...

THE WICKED WOLF!

"RUN!" cried Alice.

"All the way home!"

But Jack didn't move.

"The Wolf isn't wicked," said Jack.
"The Wolf is a mummy…
That's what the noise is!
Wolf Mummy is singing her babies
to sleep!

Look!"

Rock-a-bye babies
under the trees,

Soft is your leafbed
and gentle the breeze,

Time now to dream
sing the stars in the sky,

So sail off to sleep
on my sweet lullaby.

"Everything is all right," said Jack.
Then he gave a great big yawn.
"It's time to go home."

And he held Alice's hand.

Alice and Jack
walked back through
the forest ...

and all the way home.

They got into their
nice, warm pyjamas and
snuggled down deep.

And they sailed off to sleep
on that sweet lullaby.

TIMOTHY KNAPMAN

is a children's writer, lyricist and playwright. His children's books have been translated into fifteen languages worldwide and include *Soon*, illustrated by Patrick Benson, *Follow the Track All the Way Back*, illustrated by Ben Mantle, *Dinosaurs Don't Have Bedtimes!*, illustrated by Nikki Dyson, and *Can't Catch Me!*, illustrated by Simona Ciraolo. His titles are often featured on CBeebies Bedtime Stories. He lives in Weybridge, Surrey. Find him online at timothyknapman.co.uk and on Twitter as @TimothyKnapman.

HELEN OXENBURY is among the

most popular and critically acclaimed illustrators of all time. Her many award-winning books for children include *We're Going on a Bear Hunt*, written by Michael Rosen, *Farmer Duck*, written by Martin Waddell and *There's Going to Be a Baby*, written by John Burningham; as well as her classic board books for babies. Helen has won the prestigious Kate Greenaway Medal twice – in 1969, for

The Quangle Wangle's Hat and *The Dragon of an Ordinary Family*, and in 1999 for *Alice's Adventures in Wonderland*. She lives in London. Find her on Twitter as @HelenOxenbury.